THOMAS THE TANK ENGINE BUZZ BOOKS:

First published 1991 by Buzz Books,
an imprint of Reed International Books Ltd,
Michelin House, 81 Fulham Road, London SW3 6RB

LONDON MELBOURNE AUCKLAND

Copyright © William Heinemann 1991

All publishing rights: William Heinemann Ltd. All television
and merchandising rights licensed by William Heinemann Ltd
to Britt Allcroft (Thomas) Ltd exclusively, worldwide.

Photographs © Britt Allcroft (Thomas) Ltd 1985, 1986
Photographs by David Mitton, Kenny McArthur and
Terry Permane for Britt Allcroft's production of
Thomas the Tank Engine and Friends

ISBN 1 85591 150 7

Printed and bound in Great Britain by BPCC Hazell Books,
Paulton and Aylesbury

THOMAS COMES TO BREAKFAST

buzz books

Thomas the Tank Engine has worked his branch line for many years, and knows it very well.

"You know just where to stop, Thomas," laughed his driver. "You could almost manage it without me!"

Thomas had become conceited. He didn't realise that his driver was joking.

Later he boasted to the others. "Driver says I don't need him now."

"Don't be daft," snorted Percy.

"I'd never go without *my* driver," said Toby earnestly. "I'd be frightened."

"Pooh!" boasted Thomas. "I'm not scared."

"You'd never dare," said the other engines.

"I would then," boasted Thomas. "You'll see!"

Next morning the fireman came. Thomas drowsed comfortably in the shed as the warmth spread through his boiler. Percy and Toby were still asleep.

Thomas opened his eyes and then he suddenly remembered. "Silly stick in the muds," he chuckled. "I'll show them! Driver hasn't come yet, so here goes."

He cautiously tried one piston; then the
other. "They're moving! They're moving!"
he whispered. "I'll just go out, then I'll stop
and 'wheeesh'. That'll make them jump!"

Very, very quietly he headed past
the door.

Thomas thought that he was being clever, but really he was only moving because a careless cleaner had meddled with his controls. He soon found out his mistake.

He tried to "wheeesh" but he couldn't. He tried to stop but he couldn't. He just kept rolling along.

"The buffers will stop me!" he thought hopefully, but the siding had no buffers.

Thomas's wheels left the rails and crunched the tarmac. There was the station master's house!

Thomas didn't dare to look at what was coming next. The station master and his family were about to have breakfast.

"Horrors!" cried Thomas and shut his eyes.

There was a crash! The house rocked
and broken glass tinkled. Plaster peppered
the plates.

Thomas had collected a bush on his travels. He peered anxiously into the room through its leaves. He couldn't speak.

The station master was furious.

The station master's wife picked up her
plate. "You miserable engine," she scolded.
"Just look what you've done to our
breakfast! Now I shall have to cook
some more."

She banged the door. More plaster fell. This time, it fell on Thomas.

Thomas felt depressed. The plaster was tickly. He wanted to sneeze but he didn't dare in case the house fell on him. Nobody came for a long time. Everyone was much too busy.

At last workmen propped up the house with strong poles and laid rails through the garden.

Donald and Douglas arrived. "Dinna fash yerself, Thomas. We'll soon hae ye back on the rails," they laughed.

Puffing hard, the twins managed to haul Thomas back to safety.

Bits of fencing, the bush and a broken
window frame festooned Thomas's front,
which was badly twisted. He looked very
funny.

The twins laughed and left him.
Thomas was in disgrace, but there was
worse to come.

"You are a very naughty engine," came a voice.

"I know, sir," said Thomas. "I'm sorry, sir." Thomas's voice was muffled behind his bush.

"You must go to the works and have your front end mended. It will be a long job," said the Fat Controller.

"Yes, sir," faltered Thomas.

"Meanwhile, a diesel railcar called Daisy will do your work."

"A d-d-diesel, sir? D-D-Daisy, sir?"
Thomas spluttered.

"Yes, Thomas," said the Fat Controller.
"Diesels *always* stay in their sheds till they
are wanted. Diesels *never* gallivant off to
breakfast in station masters' houses."

The Fat Controller turned on his heels,
and sternly walked away.

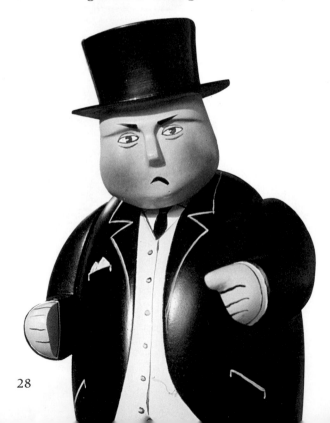